Three books
written and illustrated by

James Marshall

Fox Be Nimble

Fox Outfoxed

Fox on Stage

BARNES
&NOBLE
B O O K S
N E W   Y O R K

Reprinted by permission of

DIAL BOOKS FOR YOUNG READERS

a division of Penguin Books USA Inc.

FOX BE NIMBLE

by James Marshall

PUFFIN BOOKS

For Olivia, Nicholas, Manton,
and Thacher Hurd

The Dial Easy-to-Read logo is a registered trademark of
Dial Books for Young Readers,
a division of Penguin Books USA Inc., ® TM 1,162,718.
Fox Be Nimble
Copyright © 1990 by James Marshall
All rights reserved
Printed in the U.S.A.
For information address Dial Books for Young Readers,
a division of Penguin Books USA Inc.,
375 Hudson Street • New York, New York 10014.

FOX
THE
FAMOUS

Fox's mom was on the phone.

"Fox would *love* to help,"
said Mom.

"I'll send him right over."

"I won't do it," said Fox.

"Whatever it is.

I'm playing rock star."

"Mrs. Ling across the street needs you to sit with her kids," said Mom.

"Why don't *you* do it?" said Fox.

"This is my quiet time," said Mom. "Now hurry up."

"No," said Fox.

"And that is that."

"Oh really?" said Mom.

And Fox went across the street.

"How nice of you, Fox,"

said Mrs. Ling.

"Mom made me,"

said Fox.

Mrs. Ling got into her car.

"I do hope they behave," she said.

"I can handle them," said Fox.

"They're just kids."

Mrs. Ling drove off.

"Hot dog!" yelled the Ling kids.

And they went wild.

"Stop that!" cried Fox.

"Come down from there!" cried Fox.

"Quit it!" cried Fox.

"I don't have time for this!"

But the Ling kids would not quit.

They did just what they wanted.

Fox had to get tough.

"I'll tell your mom!" he said.

The Ling kids got very still.

"We'll be good," they said.

"Why don't you go play

in the backyard?" said Fox.

The kids liked that idea.

"May we play with our new balloons?"
they said.

"I don't see why not,"
said Fox.

Fox went back to playing rock star.
"The girls will love this," he said.

Suddenly he had an odd feeling.

The Ling kids were up to something.

Fox ran into the backyard.

"Come back here this minute!"

he cried.

"Bye-bye!" the Ling kids called out.

"Oh, no!" cried Fox.

"Their mom will *kill* me!

I'll have to catch them!"

He climbed the fence.

And he fell right into some mud,

tore his brand-new blue jeans,

tripped and stubbed his toe,

and ran smack into Mrs. O'Hara.

Then Fox got a bright idea.

He climbed up

to a very high place.

"I'll grab them when they float by,"

he said.

He tried not to look down.

Fox didn't like high places.

But the wind carried the Ling kids

right back home.

"What have you little darlings

been up to?" said Mrs. Ling.

"And just *what* have you done

with poor Fox?"

That night Fox's mom turned on the TV.

"A fox was rescued from a high place today," said the newscaster.

"Why that's *you*, Fox!" said Mom.

"Fox is famous!" cried little Louise.

"Oh, quit it!" said Fox.

FOX
THE
BRAVE

Fox stepped on one of his skates
and went flying.

"Who left *that* there?" he cried.

And he landed with a bang.

Mom and Louise came running.

"I'm dying!" cried Fox.

"It's only a scratch," said Mom.

"Nothing to worry about."

"I can't look at all the blood!"
cried Fox.

"There's no blood," said Mom.

"Don't leave me!" cried Fox.

Mom and Louise put Fox to bed.

"Call Doctor Ed," said Fox.

"Before it's too late."

"Really, Fox," said Mom.

"You're making *such* a fuss."

Louise called Doctor Ed to come over.

Then she stepped on Fox's other skate,

bounced down the stairs,

flew right out the front door,

and ran smack into Mrs. O'Hara.

"Poor Louise must hurt all over," said Doctor Ed.

But Louise didn't cry.

She didn't complain.

Not even a peep.

"Very brave," said Doctor Ed.

"Very brave."

"Louise is tough," said Mom.

"Now then," said Doctor Ed.

"What's the matter with Fox?"

"Oh, it's just a scratch," said Fox.

"I don't like to make a fuss."

Mom didn't say a word.

FOX
ON
PARADE

"Fox is showing off!"

said Dexter.

"Quit it, Fox," said Mr. Sharp.

"We don't have time for this.

The big parade is next week."

And the band played on.

"Fox is showing off again!"

said Carmen.

"That does it!" said Mr. Sharp.

Fox was told to leave the band room.
"Come back when you have
changed your ways," said Mr. Sharp.
"But I *like* to show off,"
said Fox.

Fox sat in the school yard by himself.

"There are some things

you just *can't* change," he said.

"Look out! Look out!"

cried a voice.

Fox almost got hit.

"Oh, dear!" said his friend Raisin.

"I'm *so* clumsy!"

"You should be more careful!"
said Fox crossly.

"I'm sorry," said Raisin.

"I'm just not good at this."

"It looks easy to me," said Fox.

"Oh really?" said Raisin.

"Then *you* try it."

Fox gave the baton a twirl.

And he dropped it on his toe.

"Ouch!" he yelled.

"This is harder than it looks."

But soon he got the hang of it

and he got better and better.

Raisin couldn't believe her eyes.

"Wow!" said Dexter.

"Will you look at *that*!"

"Fox," said Mr. Sharp.

"May I speak to you a moment?"

"What now?" said Fox.

On the day of the big parade

the band was great.

Fox could show off

to his heart's content.

And the crowd went wild.

48

FOX OUTFOXED

by James Marshall

PUFFIN BOOKS

For my sister, Cynthia

A
FASTER
FOX

One Saturday morning

Fox went out for some fun.

At Carmen's house

something was up.

"The Big Race is today,"

said Carmen.

Fox looked at Carmen's race car.

"Does it have an engine?" he said.

"It has pedals," said Carmen.

"That's no fun," said Fox.

"First prize in The Big Race

is a free shopping spree

at the candy store," said Carmen.

Fox ran home to build

his own race car.

"There isn't much time," he said.

"May I help?" asked Louise.

"Go away," said Fox.

Then Fox had one of his great ideas.

He ran after Louise.

"You can help," said Fox.

"But you must do as I say."

"Oh goody!" said Louise.

Fox made it to the starting line
just in the nick of time.
He looked smug.

"On your mark!" cried the starter.

"Get set! Go!"

The race was on!

9

Fox shot ahead of the others.

He was really moving!

He crossed the finish line.

But he kept right on going...

smack into Mrs. O'Hara's
pretty flower garden.
"You!" said Mrs. O'Hara.
"It wasn't my fault!"
said Fox.

Suddenly out popped Louise.

"Did I run fast enough, Fox?"

she said.

"Aha!" yelled the starter.

"Shame, shame!" cried the others.

Fox spent the rest of the day

working in Mrs. O'Hara's garden.

"I hope you learned your lesson,"

said Dexter.

But Fox was in no mood to hear *that*.

COMIC FOX

Fox had lots and lots
of comic books.

"Are you sure you have enough?"
said Mom.

"I could always use more,"
said Fox.

"I wasn't serious," said Mom.

"I couldn't live without my comics,"
said Fox.

And he took his ten best comics
to read in the yard.

"This is great," said Fox.

Just then his pretty new neighbor

Lulu came by.

"May I see?" she said.

"Sure," said Fox.

"You don't read *comics*!" said Lulu.

"They're for little kids."

"Er...they're not mine," said Fox.

"I just found them.

I was about to throw them away."

"Then you won't mind if I take them for my little brother," said Lulu.

"Er...," said Fox.

"Bye-bye," said Lulu.

And she was gone.

"My ten best comics!" cried Fox.

He felt sick all afternoon.

Later he went for a walk.

In front of Lulu's house

he couldn't believe his eyes.

Lulu was reading Fox's comics

out loud to her friends.

"These are great!"

said her friends.

"Wait until you hear *this* one!"

said Lulu.

"It's my favorite!"

"Where did you get these?"

said her friends.

"Oh," said Lulu,

"I was *very* clever."

Fox had to go home and lie down.

"Is he dying?" said Louise.

"No," said Mom.

"But he's taking it pretty hard."

FOX
OUTFOXED

Halloween was coming up.

Fox and the gang were excited.

"My costume will be really wild!"

said Carmen.

"Think of all the tricks we can pull,"

said Dexter.

"Keep your voices down,"

whispered Fox.

"We don't want any little kids

tagging along."

On Halloween Fox was ready.

He had worked hard on his costume.

"No one will ever know me," he said.

"Fox, dear," said Mom,

"Louise is all set

to go trick-or-treating."

"You're not serious!" said Fox.

"She'll just get in the way,

and her costume is *dumb*!"

"You're so mean," said Mom.

Carmen and Dexter were waiting.

"Mom made me bring Louise," said Fox.

"Little kids are trouble," said Dexter.

"I'll handle this," said Carmen.

"Now see here!" she said to Louise.

"Tonight I have magic powers.

Do not cause any problems.

Or I'll turn you into a *real* pumpkin!"

Louise didn't say a word.

"Little kids will believe *anything*,"

whispered Carmen to Fox.

They set off trick-or-treating.

Soon Dexter had an ugly thought.

"Little kids always get

the most treats," he said,

"and there won't be enough for us."

"Hmm," said Carmen.

At the corner of Cedar and Oak

they put Louise on a bench.

"Now don't you move," said Fox.

"We'll be right back."

And Louise was left all alone.

Fox and the gang went

to Mrs. O'Hara's house.

"Trick or treat!" they called out.

"Hello, Fox," said Mrs. O'Hara.

"I'd know *you* anywhere.

But where is your little sister?"

"Oh, she's around," said Fox.

Fox and the gang

went on trick-or-treating

until their bags were full.

"Let's go get Louise," said Fox.

They went back to the bench.

"Come on, Louise," said Fox.

But Louise didn't move.

"Come on, Louise!"

said Dexter and Carmen.

But Louise didn't budge.

"Oh my gosh!" cried Fox.

"It's a *real* pumpkin!"

"Wow!" said Carmen.

They went to the cops.

"My little sister got turned into

a pumpkin!" cried Fox.

"But it wasn't my fault!"

"Well, well," said Officer Bob.

"Maybe we could bake a nice pie."

"This is serious!" cried Fox.

"*Do* something!"

"I'm afraid it's too late,"

said Officer Bob.

Fox and the gang

left the police station.

On the way home

Fox tripped on his costume.

"Look out!" cried Carmen.

Fox went flying.

40

The pumpkin landed with a splat.

"Now you've done it!" said Dexter.

"Poor Louise," said Carmen.

"What a mess."

41

Fox put the pieces into a shopping bag
and ran to the hospital.

"Put Louise back together!" he cried.

"*Really,* Fox!" said Nurse Wendy.

"I don't have time for your jokes.

I've got a lot of sick people here."

Fox went home.

"Sit down, Mom," he said.

And he told her about Louise.

"That *is* too bad," said Mom.

"You're not cross?" said Fox.

"These things happen," said Mom.

"And we don't really *need* Louise."

"Don't say that!" cried Fox.

"She was always in the way," said Mom.

"Not always," said Fox.

"Would you be sweet to Louise
if we had her back?" said Mom.

"Oh, *yes*!" said Fox.

"I would even let her read my comics."

Louise flew out of the closet.

"Tra la!" she sang.

Fox nearly fainted.

"I get to read your comics!"

said Louise.

Later Fox heard Mom and Louise
talking.

"Fox really thought I turned into
a pumpkin!" said Louise.

"Big kids will believe *anything*!"

Fox went to bed very cross.

Mom came to say good night.

"I wasn't really fooled," said Fox.

"I was just playing along."

"You're so smart," said Mom.

FOX ON STAGE

by James Marshall

PUFFIN BOOKS

For Anita Lobel

FOX
ON FILM

When Grannie Fox had a bad spill

on the ski slopes,

she broke both legs.

"Grannie Fox will have to be

in the hospital for some time,"

said Doctor Ed.

"Old bones take longer to heal."

"Oh, what do *you* know?"

said Grannie.

But Doctor Ed was right.

Grannie had to stay in the hospital

for weeks and weeks.

"I'm so bored I could scream," she said.

"Grannie is down in the dumps," said Fox.

"We should do something to

pick up her spirits."

Then Fox got one of his great ideas.

"Louise and I are going to make
a video for Grannie," said Fox.
"How sweet," said Mom.
"But if anything happens to my camera..."
"I know what I'm doing," said Fox.

The next day the video was finished.

Fox's friends came for a look.

"This better be good," said Carmen.

"I'm very busy."

Fox put in the tape.

"Here I am taking out the trash," said Fox.

"This is me in my new shoes," said Fox. "Hm," said Dexter.

"Me, flossing my teeth," said Fox.

"*How* exciting," said Carmen.

"Me again," said Fox.

"So we see," said Dexter.

11

"Care to watch it again?" said Fox.

"Certainly not," said Carmen.

"You've wasted our time."

"What was wrong with it?"
said Fox.

"It was *dumb*," said Dexter.

"I liked it, Fox," said Louise.

The next day Fox tried again.

He put a new tape in the camera

and set off.

This time he left Louise at home.

"You're so mean," said Louise.

Just down the block Fox filmed

Mrs. O'Hara trying on her new corset.

"Smile!" said Fox.

"Monster!" cried Mrs. O'Hara.

And Fox tore away.

Down a dark alley

Fox filmed some bad dogs.

They were up to no good.

"Catch that fox!" they cried.

And Fox tore away.

In the park Fox saw Officer Tom

smooching with his girlfriend.

"Nice shot!" said Fox.

"You'll be sorry!" cried Officer Tom.

But Fox got away.

17

Fox went to the hospital

to show Grannie his new video.

But Grannie and Louise

were already watching one.

"This is Fox flossing his teeth,"

said Louise.

"Wow!" said Grannie.

"Don't watch that!" cried Fox.

"It's dumb!"

"What do you know?" said Grannie.

"We just *love* it."

At Fox's house some folks were waiting.

"That's him!" cried Mrs. O'Hara.

Maybe they don't like being
movie stars, thought Fox.
And he went inside to face the music.

FLYING
FOX

Fox and the gang

went to a magic show.

"I hope this guy is good,"

said Dexter.

"It's probably just a lot

of dumb tricks with scarves,"

said Fox.

"Anybody can do it."

And they sat down in

the very first row.

The lights went down.

And the curtain went up.

Mr. Yee, the World's Greatest Magician,

came forward.

"Welcome to the show,"

he said.

"Some parts will be *very* scary!"

"Oh, sure," whispered Fox.

"Let the magic begin!"

cried Mr. Yee.

First Mr. Yee did a trick with scarves.

"I told you," said Fox.

Then Mr. Yee made his helper vanish.

"Ho-hum," said Fox.

Next Mr. Yee pulled a rabbit from a hat.

"Big deal," said Fox.

Next Mr. Yee put his helper to sleep.

"This is *so* dumb," said Fox.

"What's all the chatter?" said Mr. Yee.

"It's Fox!" called out Dexter.

"You don't say," said Mr. Yee.

"Come up on stage, Fox."

"You're going to get it!" said Dexter.

Fox went up on stage.

"Sit here, Mr. Smarty," said Mr. Yee.

"Let's see how brave you are."

"Brave?" said Fox.

"Abracadabra!" said Mr. Yee.

Slowly the chair rose in the air.

"Where are the wires?" said Fox.

"No wires," said Mr. Yee.

"Only magic."

Fox held on tight.

And the chair flew all over.

"I'd like to come down," said Fox.

"Oh my," said Mr. Yee.

"I forgot how to do this part."

"Try Abracadabra!" said Fox.

"Abracadabra," said Mr. Yee.

Fox came gently down.

And the show was over.

At home Fox told Louise to sit down.

"Abracadabra!" said Fox.

The chair did not move.

"Rats!" said Fox.

"You just need practice," said Mom.

FOX
ON STAGE

One Saturday morning

Fox and his friends

were just lying around.

"What a sad little group,"

said Mom.

"Why don't you *do* something?"

"The television is broken,"

said Fox.

"Oh, that *is* terrible!"

said Mom.

Then Fox had one of his

great ideas.

"Let's put on a play!" he said.

"We can charge everyone a dime."

"We'll get rich!" said Dexter.

"I'll buy a new car," said Carmen.

And they went to the library.

"Let's do a spooky play," said Carmen.

"We can scare all the little kids."

"Here's what you need," said Miss Pencil.

"It's called *Spooky Plays*.

My favorite is 'The Mummy's Toe.'"

"Oooh," said the gang.

Fox and the gang went home to practice.

"The Mummy's Toe" was *very* scary.

Dexter played the mummy.

Carmen was the princess.

And Fox was the hero.

Soon things were moving right along.

Fox and Dexter worked hard

on the set.

And Carmen put up posters

all over town.

Mom and Louise helped out

with the costumes.

"Hold still," said Mom.

"I hope I'm scary enough," said Dexter.

It was time for the play.

Fox peeked out from behind the curtain.

There was a big crowd.

"I hope everything goes okay,"

said Dexter.

"What could go wrong?" said Fox.

The curtain went up.

And the play began.

Right away Carmen forgot her lines.

"Well I *did* know them,"

she said to the audience.

Then Dexter crashed through

the scenery.

"Whoops," said Dexter.

It was Fox's turn

to appear.

Suddenly it began to rain.

Fox's beautiful paper costume

fell apart in front of everyone.

"What do we do now?" said Carmen.

"Pull the curtain down!"

Fox called out to Louise.

And Louise pulled with all her might.

The curtain came down.

"Who turned out the lights?"

cried Carmen.

"Where am I?" said Dexter.

"The play is ruined!" cried Fox.

"*Everything* went wrong!"

The next day

Fox heard some folks talking.

"That Fox really knows how
to put on a funny show," someone said.
"Funniest thing I ever saw,"
said someone else.

And Fox began to plan his next show.